Investi GATORS

Take the Plunge

written and illustrated by

John Patrick Green

with colour by **Aaron Polk**

MACMILLAN CHILDREN'S BOOKS

To my biggest fan.

Wait, scratch that... To my air conditioner.

First published 2020 by First Second

This edition published in the UK 2021 by Macmillan Children's Books
an imprint of Pan Macmillan
The Smithson, 6 Briset Street, London EC1M 5NR
EU representative: Macmillan Publishers Ireland Limited,
Mallard Lodge, Lansdowne Village, Dublin 4
Associated companies throughout the world
www.panmacmillan.com

ISBN 978-1-5290-6606-7

A CIP catalogue record for this book is available from the British Library.

Cover design by John Patrick Green and Kirk Benshoff
Interior book design by John Patrick Green
Interior colour by Aaron Polk

Printed in China by Leo Paper

MIX
Paper from
responsible sources
FSC® C116313
FSC
www.fsc.org

Chapter 1
INVESTIGATORS!

Brash! We're getting a message from S.U.I.T.* headquarters!

MANGO and **BRASH**, this is the **General Inspector!** I have an urgent mission for you! A *rocket* is about to launch from a secret base beneath the opera house!

Your job is to go undercover as orchestra musicians—

Way ahead of you, boss!

*Special Undercover Investigation Teams

We're already on the case!

On the *rocket*, to be more accurate. I left my trombone case backstage.

Ah, wonderful! That's why you're our **TOP AGENTS!**

That rocket carries **stolen code** that could turn any machine into a **COMBINOTRON** – a device that can *stick any two things together!*

You mean like duct tape?

2

Worse than duct tape! Or *better*, depending on how you look at it... Like most technology, a **combinotron** could be used for good *or* evil! For example: If you combine **shoes** with **wheels**, you'll make some fun roller skates. And fun is **GOOD**.

But if you combine **broccoli** with **lollipops**? YOU'LL RUIN CANDY! And that's **BAD**.

If that code found its way into someone's microwave oven, instead of *heating* things it would *COMBINE* them! Who knows what—

Hello, Gators!

Oh, hi, C-ORB*!

*Computerized Ocular Remote Butler

3

Guess who has two thumbs and is going on a mission of their own? **ME!**

That's great, C-ORB! Did you hear that, Brash?

MANGO! We're on a **ROCKET!** This is no time for idle chitchat!

Brash is right! InvestiGators, do whatever it takes to make sure the **combinotron code** on that rocket doesn't fall into the *wrong hands!*

Don't worry, boss! We'll **GATOR DONE!**

Welp, won't need *this* anymore.

TOSS

vvrp

CRASH

TWANG

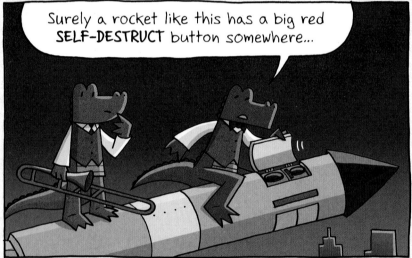

Uh...did that do anything?

Shouldn't there be, like, a countdown?

Whoops.

"Whoops," what?

Oh, I'm sure it's nothing...

SELF-DESTRUCT

TRANSMIT CODE

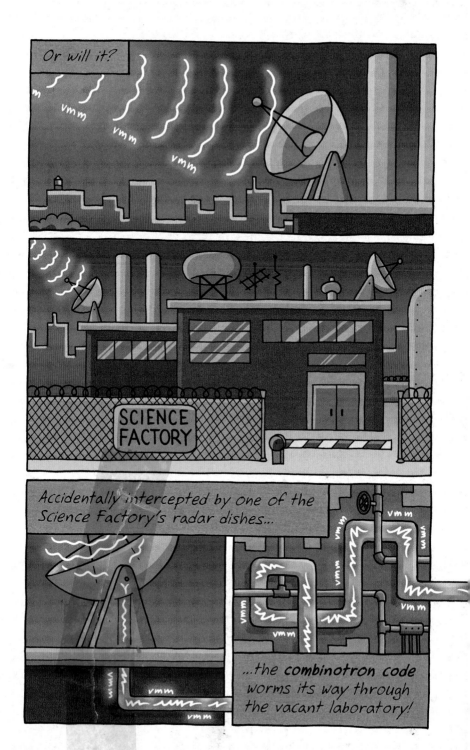

```
Installing New Code. Recompiling Hug Subroutine...
[
function HUGS() == function COMBINOTRON()
    if Command = HUG;
        set Hands(COMBINE)
hugs=combine  hUgS=cOmBiNe  HUGS=COMBINE

***INSTALLATION COMPLETE***
```

These are the **WRONG HANDS** indeed!

Chapter 2

That was the scene moments ago when a rocket *rudely* interrupted a performance at the opera house!

BREAKING NEWS: Opera House Hosts Rock(et) Concert

This is Cici Boringstories reporting for *Action News Now.* Capturing the destruction from above is the *Action News Now* helicopter in the sky!

One thing's for sure, Cici... that rocket brought the house *DOWN!*

Rumor has it this rocket carried code that could be used to program a **COMBINOTRON**... whatever *that* is!
How or why there is a rocket base beneath the opera house, or where this rocket was going, is still unknown. But amazingly enough, it was destroyed by...

...this trombonist and violinist, who fortunately were wearing parachutes underneath their tuxedos!

Hello!

If I, **CRACKERDILE**, had the ability to program a COMBINOTRON, all my problems would be *solved!*

Because in my current cracker state, I'm in danger of being *DIS*solved!

I may still possess the strength of a giant saltine, but with a **combinotron** I could *merge* myself with something *MUCH* stronger.

Like...wood... or brick...

NO, *METAL!*

Yes, metal! Metal is **much** stronger than cracker.

Then I could FINALLY get rid of those InvestiGators and have my revenge.

Yes, I know who you are, **MANGO** and **BRASH**. You're not professional musicians! You're a *Special Undercover Investigation Team!*

And those parachutes came from your V.E.S.T.s! You **never** would've stopped that rocket if you didn't have your *Very Exciting Spy Technology.*

Without all the gadgets in those V.E.S.T.s, you'd be *normal* alligators...

...just as I was once a *normal* crocodile.

But that was before I got *crackerized*. When I, too, was an Agent of S.U.I.T.

If only I still had a V.E.S.T. of my own.

Now that I think of it, if I had a *new* V.E.S.T. I'd be evenly matched against those InvestiGators. And as a former agent, I know exactly how to get into **S.U.I.T. headquarters** — via the sewers!

I can break in, **STEAL** a V.E.S.T., and have all the gadgets it contains at my disposal!

Hmm, no... That won't work.

In my current crackery condition, I'm too weak to risk it.

All they'd have to do is turn on the sprinkler system and I'd get soggy. Like cereal left in milk for too long!

I wouldn't even make it *that* far. I'd get drenched just trying to sneak in through the toilets!

Ironic that I've taken up residence in this damp sewer, but I'm a crocodile, and you go with what you know.

Plus, rent for an *evil lair* in this city is *sky high!*

20

If I can't get a V.E.S.T. for myself, then I'll do the next best thing... I'll form my OWN team of agents to **oppose** S.U.I.T.!

We'll be called...
The Opposuits!

Ha, ha, ha!
PERFECT!

Oh, wait. That name's taken. Turns out it's an **opossum ska band!**

What's the point of a team without a good name? Let's see, can't use *SUIT*... Maybe PANTS? No. Socks? Hmm... Blazers?

Yes! **BLAZERS!** Hot like *FIRE*, but also another word for *jacket!*

The **BLAZERS!** Whose mission is...the *Total Annihilation of Idiot Law-doers!*

That's it! **T.A.I.L.!** I even have a tail!

BLAZER *T.A.I.L.S!*

Wait, that doesn't sound quite right—

Chapter 3

The next morning...

...Milk, juice, and one flapjack wacky stack.

Yours will be out shortly.

Thanks.

Finally, **DINNER!**

What? Mango, it's *breakfast* time.

Exactly! Breakfast is the most important meal of the day. Which is why I also eat breakfast for LUNCH and DINNER.

Okaaay...

Shlorp

But since we were stuck in a tree all night, I missed out on yesterday's dinner.

So now I'm having last night's breakfast dinner for breakfast today!

You want some, Brash? It's got pumpkin, rhubarb, jelly beans, garbanzo beans, baked beans—

No, thanks. I'll wait for my chilaquiles.

As usual, the fastest way to get to S.U.I.T. headquarters is to **flush** ourselves into the sewer!

VVVRNT!

Huh?

WARNING! CODE S.O.U.P.

"Warming cold soup"?

No, it's a warning! S.O.U.P. stands for *S.U.I.T.'s Other Underground Passages.*

WARNING! CODE S.O.U.P.

A **CODE S.O.U.P.** means secret entrances like the sewers have been compromised!

We'll have to find *another* way into S.U.I.T. HQ! C'mon, Mango!

BUMP!

You two aren't trying to **dine and dash**, are you?

Whaaat? Brash, *dash?* **NEVER!**

Mm-hmm.

Well, here's your chilaquiles. *And* your bill.

Aw, that breakfast looks *sooooo* good... But there's just not enough time to sit down and eat it!

Get it to go! You can eat it in a montage!

YO, CHUCK! HIT ME WITH A TAKEAWAY BAG!

Thank you!

Chapter 4

Meanwhile...

SCIENCE
FACTORY

Morning, boss!

WELCOME to the WORLD of SCIENCE!

EXIT

Good morning!

Ooh, it's the Head Scientist!

He's so *scientisty!*

Lookin' good, fellow scientists!

Ooh, let's see what's on the lunch menu...

CAFETERI

TODAY'S SPECIAL
MON
TUE
WED
THU
FRI

Today's **HOT DOG DAY!** Tasty tubes of meat! How exciting!

TODAY'S SPECIAL
MON
TUE
WED
THU
FRI

Ah! Morning, Dr. Doodledoo!

Mornin', bruh!

CAFETERIA

C

THURSDAY IS CHICKEN FINGER DAY?!!

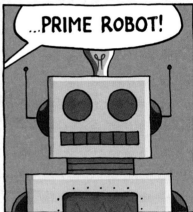

Did you say something?

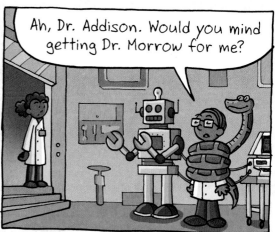

Ah, Dr. Addison. Would you mind getting Dr. Morrow for me?

Anything I can help you with?

Sally, you're a **botanist**. If I were stuck in a tree, *maybe* I'd need a *plant doctor*.

But I am caught by a *SNAKE*, and therefore need a **SERPENTOLOGIST**.

HISS!

FINE, I'll get Thomas.

Well, if you want to see some *real* hugging, then let me introduce you to **PRIME ROBOT!**

The first robot to feel and express **TRUE HUMAN EMOTIONS!**

May I ask... *why?*

Why? If I asked myself "*WHY* make this? *WHY* make that?" I'd **NEVER** get any science done!

Instead of asking "why," I say, "why not?"

HE—LLO—SAL—AD.

Salad? Really?

His language skills will improve the more we talk to him. But let's move on...

tap tap

Thomas, with your permission?

As you'd say, why not?

Prime Robot, **hug** Dr. Morrow.

HUG—MOR—ROW.

Uh...

```
iF Command = HUG;
    set Hands(COMBINE)
hUgs=combine    hUgs=ComBinE
HUgs=cOMbiNe    huGs=cOMbiNe
hUGs=ComBinE    HUgs=cOMBinE
HUGs=cOMBINE    hUgs=ComBinE
HUGs=COMBInE    HUGS=COMBINE
HUGs=COMBINE    HUGS=cOMBINe
HUGs=COMBINE    HUGS=COMBINE
HUGS=COMB...
```

Chapter 5

Finally, inside S.U.I.T. headquarters...

C'mon, Brash!

We're almost at the General Inspector's office!

I think I ate too fast during the montage. I could really use a bathroom.

Why didn't you go before we left?

I didn't have to go **then!**

General Inspector? I was expecting C-ORB to greet us.

That's why you're here, Gators.

This is **Agent Monocle**. She built C-ORB and monitors the robot's activity.

Last night, during C-ORB's mission, I lost contact.

Please hold all questions till the end.

I don't think I **can** hold it. May I be excused?

I'm afraid you will **have** to hold it, Agent Brash.

Go on, Monocle.

Before I sent C-ORB into the sewer, I thought Crackerdile's goose was cooked—

It was! *LITERALLY!* By Chef Gustavo, who re-baked him!

Well, as evidenced by the last video I received from the unit, C-ORB has fallen into Crackerdile's hands.

We believe he plans to **break into** S.U.I.T. headquarters.

And since *Crackerdile* is Brash's former partner, *Daryl*, he would obviously remember any sneaky ways in.

Hence the cold soup – *I MEAN* – Code S.O.U.P.

The secret sewer systems *you* use to get into HQ have been **sealed off.** Therefore, all the bathrooms are **closed for business!**

But I've got so much *business* to do!

Unfortunately, C-ORB's tracking device has been disabled, but we *do* know its last recorded location when it was turned off.

C-ORB TRAKR

We *can't* have S.U.I.T. technology in the wrong hands. **GATORS!** Go into the sewers to retrieve C-ORB. And, if possible, *capture Crackerdile!*

Can't we just *FLUSH* him out? He's still made of normal cracker dough, so even a *little* bit of water should be enough to stop him.

Like a witch!

What, none of you have seen *The Wizard of Oz?*

Flushing the sewers *could* work, Agent Brash, but the only way to be sure we got him would be to flush the **WHOLE SYSTEM**...

...and that would *flood the entire city!* Including S.U.I.T. headquarters!

CATASTROPHIC FLOOD!

Under no circumstances are you to flush the system. Even as a last resort!

Brash, I can see you're anxious about this mission—

No, I just really gotta pee! And... stuff.

*Apparel Research and Manufacturing... Something

Chapter 6

I'm not anxious. **Feh!**

What he calls *anxiety*, I call a **full bladder!**

Just go behind a bush or something.

DO YOU SEE ANY BUSHES AROUND HERE, MANGO?!

Here we are! The A.R.M.S. Division.

And there's **Sven Septapus**, the lead designer!

A.R.M.S.

APPAREL RESEARCH and MANUFACTU

Hey, Sven!

AH, Mango and Brash. I've been expecting you. Let's get you fitted for your new V.E.S.T.s!

These are Agents **Fur** and **Five**. They will take your measurements.

Hi, Fur. Hi, Five.

Hi, Fur...

...and **HIGH FIVE!**

SLAP

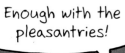

Your new V.E.S.T.s are ready, Gators! Let's take a look at all the features.

In addition to the standard equipment on all S.U.I.T. V.E.S.T.s, you'll have *everything* you could possibly need for your mission as undercover plumbers.

Ooh, snorkels! I've always wanted to go snorkeling...

Check out the coral reef, swim with some fishies, get a tan on the beach...

This vacation's gonna be *awesome*! I don't think we'll need the *mop*, though—

MANGO, this isn't a **VACATION**! We're going into the sewer to *save C-ORB*!

Oh, right.

Then let's get these V.E.S.T.s on!

TA-DA! Ready to go, Brash?

I've been ready to *go* since we got here!

TO THE SEWERS!

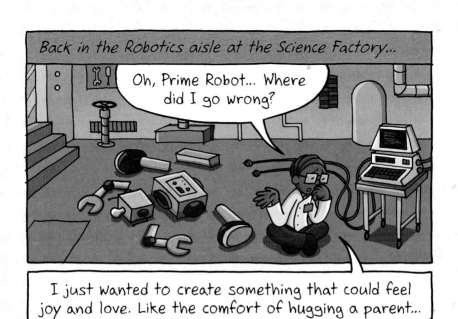

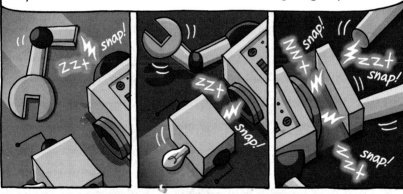

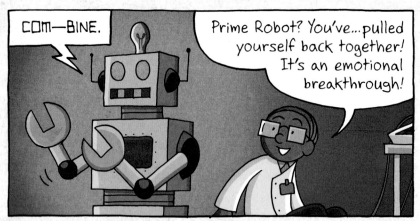

COM—BINE.

Prime Robot? You've...pulled yourself back together! It's an emotional breakthrough!

HUGS. COM—BINE—HUGS.

Combine hugs? ⊰GASP!⊱ Your programming had **weird code** in it that said something about combining hugs!

I forgot all about it when I got distracted by Dr. Morrow's anaconda!

YES. MOR—ROW. HUG MOR—ROW. HUG MOR— MOR—MOR—

Drat! I can't separate the *bad* code from the *good!* I'll have to delete his entire hugging subroutine!

THERE!

HUG ROUTINE: >>DELETED<<

I—MUST—HUG MORE!!

zzt

What? *No*, Prime Robot! Hug *LESS!*

Why didn't deleting the code work?

ROBOTICS SER

HUG MORE!!!

AAAH! It's the Head Scientist's emotional robot! It's gonna attack us with its *FEELINGS!*

HUG MORE!

Is "terrorized" an emotion?!

I don't know, but *RUN FOR YOUR LIFE!*

I—WANT—MORE—HUGS!

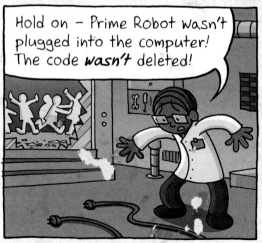

Hold on — Prime Robot wasn't plugged into the computer! The code *wasn't* deleted!

That means... he'll *never. STOP. HUGGING.*

Chapter 7

Meanwhile, in Crackerdile's lair...

If I reprogram this spy-ball to work for **ME**, I can use it to infiltrate S.U.I.T. headquarters...

...and have it steal a V.E.S.T. without anyone noticing!

Then I'll have both a V.E.S.T. and the perfect recruit for my **Blazer** team – *YOWCH!*

Curses! If only my crumby cracker fingers weren't so clumsy – huh?

GAH! Those **InvestiGators** are here! I *knew* they'd be on my tail sooner or later. I could almost *feel* it.

ZOOM

Wait, I *CAN* feel it—

RATS! Why am I so delicious? *Shoo!*

Those Gators will find me before I can finish reprogramming this thing. And without a *distraction*, I'll never escape.

Hmm... I've got an idea!

It's risky, but you may still come in handy, spy-ball...

click

twist

Time for **Plan B**...

...which stands for "Better get outta here while I can!"

Just around a U-bend...

You seem nervous, Brash.

MAP

Which is understandable, since Crackerdile was once your partner, Daryl.

But you left him for dead when he fell into a vat of **radioactive saltine dough**...

...and now he's evil and wants revenge.

We're here to *find* him, but you're worried you've *lost* your friend forever.

I–I'm **NOT** nervous... I just still need to go to the bathroom!

Well, don't go here... This place is *filthy!*

It really *would* be easiest to just *flush* the entire sewer system. Then all our problems would be *washed away!*

MANGO, **LOOK!**

C-ORB's tracking device has been reactivated!

The signal is coming from the sewer's Central Control Junction!

This way, Brash! *Hurry!*

CENTRAL CONTROL →

I'm moving as fast as I can!

Shortly...

CENTRAL CONTROL JUNCTION

C-ORB!

69

HA HA HA! Looks like my plan worked!

Now let's hope it was worth sacrificing that spy-ball!

rumble

Time to head to higher ground!

SCREECH

HIGH GROUND
ROOFTOP RESTAURANT
"The Tallest Taste in Town"
Just 97 floors up!

That'll do.

Chapter 8

Across town...
SCIENCE FACTORY
rrrrRRRrrruuUUmmMmble
Hey, you hear that rumbling?
Oh, that's just my tummy. It's excited for HOT DOG DAY!
pat pat
Or is it?
We're going in circles!
HUG MORE! HUG MORE!
rumble
QUICK! Let's hide in the snake aisle!

All over the city, the flood's effects are felt...

Water fountains...

slurp

Park fountains...

quack

quack

quack

WAAK!

WAAK!

WAAK!

Drink fountains...

SODA

Aw yeah, free refills!

SODA

...and ever since, I've lived this double life as both a doctor *AND* a copter! I'm **DOCTOR COPTER!**

Did you say...you were bitten by a radioactive news helicopter?

A *RABID* helicopter, Doc. What do you think this is, a comic book?

And now, whenever you see something *newsworthy*...you uncontrollably transform—

From mild-mannered brain surgeon **Dr. Jake Hardbones** into the *Action News Now* helicopter in the sky!

What is going on outside?!

The whole city is flooding!!

Oh! That certainly *is* newsworthy!

twitch

Can't STOP MUST REPORT!

NEWS

CHEE CHU CHEE CHOO CHUK

Well! Either I need new windows, or I need new glasses!

Breaking news! This is Cici Boringstories with the *Action News Now* headlines!

Bathing suit season's come early this year...

WATER PREDICAMENT!

...because the entire city is *flooded!*

WATER PREDICAMENT!

Is this what they call *STREAMING VIDEO?*

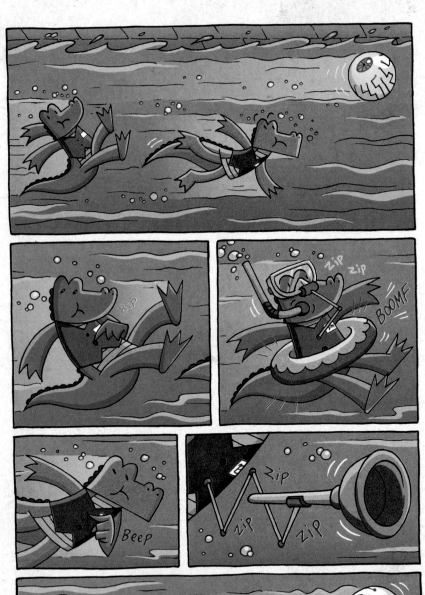

THAT didn't go as planned. But at least we recovered C-ORB. Or *E-ORB*, I guess.

Hopefully Monocle can reprogram E-ORB to not be *evil* anymore.

Chapter 9

Back at S.U.I.T. headquarters...

A-team? More like **ACCIDENT** team! You two have messed things **UP** and let me **DOWN**.

The *entire city* was flooded! **Even this office!** The water may have receded, but it came all the way up to my sock drawer.

There's nothing I hate more than *soggy socks!* Except for crime and villainy – **BUT SOGGY SOCKS COME CLOSE!**

I'm afraid I have NO CHOICE but to take you off active duty.

What?! Why? We *DID* our duty!

ESPECIALLY Brash!

We accomplished our mission to rescue C-ORB!

Yes, and according to C-ORB, you then *pushed the flood control lever*, flushing the entire system.

Which you were specifically instructed **NOT** to do!

But that's not true! C-ORB – *I MEAN* – **E**-ORB pushed that lever!

C-ORB was *reprogrammed* to be **EVIL!** Clearly it was a trap set by *Daryl!*

Brash, you have to accept that Daryl is GONE. *Literally!* Because *you* let Crackerdile get away!

I think this case has become too personal for you.

But—

So another team will take over your current investigations. I just can't have agents out there who are so...*emotional.*

I wasn't emotional. I had indigestion!

You are both hereby stripped of rank. But you **won't** be stripped of your *undercover plumber* V.E.S.T.s...

...because you'll need **them** to clean up the bathrooms in the lower levels.

Mango and Brash, you are no longer AGENTS of S.U.I.T. – you're **JANITORS!**

DISMISSED!

I believe you, Gators. But until I get C–ORB *un-evil*, the General Inspector won't see eye to eye with me.

Thanks, Monocle.

Look on the bright side, Brash. We're finally going to a bathroom!

I DON'T **NEED** TO GO ANYMORE, MANGO!

Would you like a bun-less hot dog?

No, thanks! I've got a job to do. I'm here to SNAKE a DRAIN!

I'M the serpentologist around here. What does a *plumber* know about *snakes?*

Bill

HA HA! Not *YOUR* kind of snake.

THIS kind! This tool is a **DRAIN SNAKE.** It *twists* and *slithers* through pipes to unclog them. We plumbers get pretty attached to our drain snakes. I've named mine "Slinker!"

Well, I *guess* it sounds like you know what you're doin'.

Uh, thanks.

Shouldn't you have told him about the anaconda that's loose in there?

He'll be fine. He just said he knows all about snakes! Here, have a soggy doggy.

Hard pass. **I'M** a vegetarian.

Let's see, the aisle of Dr. Morrow... *Ha!* That almost sounds scary!

BOTANY   ROBOTICS   SERPENTOLOGY

Burble

ZZt

ZZt ZZt

Looks like that should do it.

Good job, Slinker—

AAAH!! A GHOST!

?

No, not you...

Chapter 10

FREEZE, Pick Nick!

Cheese it! It's the **CROPS!**

BANK

Mango, *WHAT* are you watching?

It's **COLE'S LAW!** The only crime drama about a head of *cabbage* who's also a *cop!*

You're **supposed** to be **mopping.**

I am! But why mop *HARD* when I can mop *SMART?*

ATTENTION! *B-team*, report for duty. REPEAT! **B-TEAM**, report for duty!

B-Team. *Feh!* **WE** should be reporting for duty. And if anyone should be cleaning this up, it's *E-ORB!*

We interrupt **Cole's Law** for the Action News Now *headlines!*

Ugh, **ALWAYS** during my favorite shows!

This is Cici Boringstories, reporting *live* outside the **Science Factory**, where there's been *yet another* science accident: All the hot dog buns got *soaked*, **ruining** hot dog day!

Of greater concern, a **MONSTER** has escaped from the aisle of Dr. Morrow! I probably should've led with that.

So **WATCH OUT**, viewers!

I bet that's where the B-team is headed.

BRASH! What if this *MONSTER* was actually Crackerdile stealing some *SCIENCE?!*

Boop

The B-team doesn't have what it takes to stop Crackerdile. *ESPECIALLY* if he's stolen some science!

But...we're not AGENTS anymore. We may as well have been *kicked out* of S.U.I.T.!

Never mind that! We can't let Crackerdile slip through S.U.I.T.'s fingers — *our* fingers — again!

You're... You're right, Mango. And this could be our chance to regain the General Inspector's trust! Forget the *CODE S.O.U.P.*...

...TO THE BATHROOM!

We're already in a bathroom, aren't we?

Convenient! We can flush ourselves down the toilet and get to the Science Factory *lickety-split!*

PLEASE don't use "lick" and "toilet" in the same sentence, Mango.

PLONK

Hey, at least we know it's clean.

FLUSH

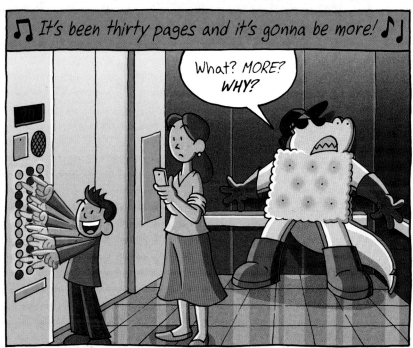

GASP! It's **BONGO** and **MARSHA**! The *B-TEAM!*

Keep out of sight, Mango! If Bongo or Marsha see us, they'll **rat** us out to the General Inspector!

But Brash, they're not *RATS*, they're *BADGERS*.

How'd they even get here so fast?

It all began with the Head Scientist's latest invention, **Prime Robot**...

Can I listen?

Shh.

What are they saying?

SHHHH!!

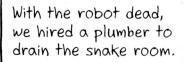

With the robot dead, we hired a plumber to drain the snake room.

But I forgot to tell him about the anaconda loose in there. And by "forgot" I mean "chose not to"!

When we went back to check on the plumber, he had the anaconda...*FOR AN ARM!*

The *plumber*...and the *snake*...had been... **COMBINED!**

?!

And this robot was nowhere to be seen?

YES! I mean, NO! It *WAS* to be seen. Seen *THROUGH!*

While helping the plumber, I turned and saw the *ghostly form* of Prime Robot, come back to **haunt** us!

But then, in a flash...

...it *disappeared* into a plug socket!

ZZZAP!

What happened next? And where's the plumber now?

Yo! This is the *best part*, bruh!

When they brought the plumber out, that snake arm went *BERSERK!*

It latched on to a streetlamp like a **grappling hook**...

...and then swung away like some sorta **superhero!**

It was **AWESOME**, yo! Like straight out of a comic book!

...comic... book...

Thank you. If you think of anything else, contact us with these Badger-brand business cards.

S.U.I.T.
BONGO and MARSHA
THE B-TEAM
"We're ready to B-lieve you"

Just press that button and we'll come to you. You don't even need a phone!

Hmm...

Hey, how come *WE* don't have fancy business cards?

Brash?

Hmph!

Beep

No mention of Crackerdile, but it sounds like his flood has caused more problems than we thought! A robot went haywire, and a plumber and an anaconda have *COMBINED* into some sort of **snake-armed monster!**

tap
tap
tap

Combined... Combined... Why does that sound familiar? Ah, well. Must be nothing.

Mango? What are you doing?

tap tap tap

zip

If we're gonna be a step ahead of Bongo and Marsha, we have to figure out what **drives** these monsters...

The bus? Taxis? Their mums?

No, Mango. What's their *motivation?* What do they **WANT?**

What *could* a snake plumber and robot ghost **WANT?** And why would Crackerdile want to make them?

If Crackerdile has taught us anything about **things** combined with **other** things...

...they all want **REVENGE!**

But what Crackerdile **really** wants is off this elevator!

This better not be another musical sequence!

Top floor.

FINALLY!

PLEASE WAIT TO BE SEATED

HA HA HA! Look at that *moist mayhem* down below.

Good thing I'm in a restaurant.

Nothing makes me hungry like doing evil!

HIGH GROUND

Chapter 11-ish

Later that night...

Home again, home again, jiggety-jig.

flik

Hello, *Home Snakes!* Sorry I'm late. I hope you're not jealous of the *Work Snakes!*

Been a long day. A long day of eating **BUN-LESS HOT DOGS!**

And yet...I'm still hungry for more...

Ah! A **banana**!

This'll satisfy my craving for more tube-shaped food!

Now let's see what kinda pickle that villain Pick Nick has gotten into on the latest episode of *Cole's Law!*

click

Huh?

DANG IT!

click click click

116

All this *science* and TV remotes still rely on *batteries*!

Wha— **THE ROBOT GHOST!**

HUG **ME!**

STAY BACK! I've got a **bananaaAAAAAAAA!!!**

We may not have a gatormobile, but neither does the B-team!

And since *they* don't use the sewer systems to get around town, we'll get to this scientist *first!*

We can do our **InvestiGatoring** and leave the scene before those badgers even get there!

Exactly!

Here we are. I'm gonna make sure the coast is clear.

Well, well, well, what do we have here?

A is better than **B**, anyway. That's why **A** comes *first* in the alphabet!

Well, we *GOT* here first, so *THIS* time **A** comes *SECOND!*

phpblrbphbrr

Weren't you two kicked out of S.U.I.T. because of the mess you made?

And aren't you supposed to be mopping it up?

THAT wasn't our fault! *CRACKERDILE* is the one who—

Mango, enough.

Look, we're all on the same side here. But you're right, this is *YOUR* case.

Bongo, Marsha, we'll follow your lead.

Technically you Gators shouldn't follow us *ANYWHERE*, but we'll let it slide...**THIS** time.

Hello?

Dr. Morrow? Are you all right?

I'm...
I'm...

I'M A BANANA!

WHAT HAPPENED?

Were you attacked by the snake-armed man?

N–NO! It was the **ROBOT GHOST!** It came out of my TV and then lunged at me!

There was a flash of light and I must have passed out. When I came to, the Robot Ghost was gone, but I discovered I had...*BANANA HANDS!*

They have a certain APPEAL.

JINX!

Do you know how hard it is to get a *BUSINESS CARD* out of your pocket with *BANANA HANDS?!*

It's hard to even **SAY** "bandana bands!"

Bonanza fans...
Band-Aid brands...
Bandolier pans...

Man, that phrase is tough. YOU try to say it.

Sultana brans.

Benedict Cumberhands... Cabana cans... Savannah sands... Pajama pants—

ENOUGH ABOUT THE BARBARIAN CLANS!
Oh, that *is* hard to say.

We've got a *MYSTERY* to solve!

Dr. Morrow, you say the Robot Ghost attacked you. Then when you awoke, you were drenched in sweat and had...barbecue...barometer...blueberry—

Banana hands.

Thank you.

And yeah, now that you mention it, I guess I *am* all sweaty. Huh.

And this same robot tried to attack you and the other scientists *BEFORE* it became a ghost?

Correct! Well, *technically* it was trying to **HUG** us. But we all ran away.

And now it's come back to taunt you—

"Haunt."

—by giving you...

...fruity fists?

Banana hands.

Hey, I said it!

This robot wants those hugs so bad it's come back from the *dead!* It has powers no one could *possibly* have seen coming!

And ghosts are *already* hard to see!

Bleep Blurp Bleep

OH, NO! That other scientist must need our help!

Blurp Bleep

Hey, wait a minute! Why is *YOUR* V.E.S.T. going off, too?

Bleep

Uh, *NO*, it's not. What are you talking about? I didn't hack your business card. That's ridiculous! Where'd you hear that? **Absurd!** Who told you?

murp murp

126

Shortly...

Oh, no! Are we too late?

Doctor! Doctor!

We're not doctors, we're paramedics!

Though I am going to night school...

Not YOU, *HER!*

Doctor...Sally Addison? The botanist?

You're... *a SALAD!*

Yes, it's me. Sally Addison, the plant doctor.

Ironically, I've somehow been *COMBINED* with the salad I was eating for dinner.

And you're all wet!

You know, you really shouldn't use so much salad dressing.

I didn't! I eat my salads **DRY**, like nature intended!

It was the **ROBOT GHOST** that got me all wet!

Riiight...

It came out of my lamp and attacked me! But really I blame HOT DOG DAY. I wouldn't even have been eating that late-night salad if there'd been a vegetarian lunch option!

Came out of a *lamp?* Like a *genie?*

No, just a normal lamp.

HONK!

That's a *tomato,* not a CLOWN NOSE!

I'm sorry, but we should really get her to the hospital. **STAT!**

The rush isn't for **her**, you know — just that we want to get back home to watch the rest of *COLE'S LAW.*

Bongo, Marsha... Mango and I will ride along with Dr. Salad in the ambulance. You badgers follow in your balloon.

Nuh-uh. **WE'LL** ride in the ambulance.

Listen, Gators, we've got it from here.

It's obvious this **ROBOT GHOST** is nothing more than an electrical appliance malfunction that turns people into whatever food they're eating.

I dunno... That doesn't sound right. I think the four of us should keep working together. The **A** *and* **B** teams.

The **Abs Team!**

We don't need your help. Just accept that we cracked this one without you.

So you Gators can crawl back to the sewers or go mop up the bathrooms or whatever.

Hey, that really hurts. I thought we were making a connection, Marsha.

I'M Bongo. **SHE'S** Marsha!

If that's the B-team, I don't wanna meet the C-team!

What should we do now, Brash?

Well, we're clearly not going to just drop this case – those two **obviously** came to the wrong conclusion.

Let's think about this...

What have we learned about the Robot Ghost so far?

It's out for revenge... comes out of electrical appliances... Uh...turns people into food...

Food...?

THAT'S IT! We forgot all about the **snake-armed monster!**

The plumber?

Right! How'd he get a **snake** on his arm?

If Dr. Morrow and Dr. Addison merged with their food because of the Robot Ghost, then the plumber-snake merger must *also* be because of the Robot Ghost!

But... that plumber wasn't going to *eat* the snake—**OH!** But maybe the *snake* was going to eat the *plumber?*

No, no, forget the FOOD part, Mango. The B-Team's wrong about the Robot Ghost turning people *into* food.

My guess is the Robot Ghost **combined** them with their *food* only because that's what they were *holding* or *touching* at the time.

Morrow's banana was in his hands... Addison's salad was tossed in her face...

135

So the snake must have been in *contact* with the plumber!

Correct! And the Robot Ghost attacked *them* just as it would later attack the scientists!

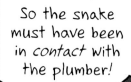

CONTACT!

Robots are supposed to be good at adding **numbers** together, not adding **RANDOM THINGS** together! How did it get these powers?

I have an idea of who might know...

...and they may *also* be Robot Ghost's next victim: the robot's creator, the **Head Scientist!**

Chapter 12, probably

Meanwhile, still hiding out high and dry...

HIGH GROUND

These nuts are making me thirsty!

But I just ≥*munch*≤ keep ≥*scarf*≤ eating them!

MY CABBAGES!

Would you like some water?

NO! Water's the **LAST** thing I need!

Sir, you've had two dozen bowls of free peanuts. If you're not going to order anything, we'll have to ask you to leave.

BAH! FINE, I'll leave. It's probably dry enough outside by now, anyway.

We interrupt **another** episode of *COLE'S LAW* for **more** *Action News Now* headlines!

What's this?

FDA SAYS NO WAY

ACTION NEWS — BREAKING REPORT

This is Cici Boringstories reporting from the hospital, where multiple patients seem to have been bizarrely transformed into food!

WITNESS the incomprehensible **DOCTOR SALAD!**

GAZE UPON the unpronounceable **BANANA HANDS!**

According to one patient, a **robot** came out of a **lamp** and turned her into a salad! So be on the lookout for a culprit matching THIS drawing by the *Action News Now* sketch artist.

Ghost? Genie? Who knows?!

ARTIST'S RENDERING

Came out of a lamp, eh? *Wait a minute...* **GENIES** aren't real! A robot *ghost*, however...*WOULD* be able to travel through plug sockets! Something tells me this robot is more than meets the eye.

Ghost? Genie? Who knows?!

It would make the *perfect* addition to my team! Why should **I** break into S.U.I.T. to steal a V.E.S.T. when I could get this **ROBOT GHOST** to do it for me?

BROCCOLI 99

Now back to the Crops and Robbers marathon.

NOTHING WILL BE ABLE TO STOP ME!

shuf

shuf

shuf

You gonna clean up all those peanut shells?

NOPE!

'Cause I'm *EVIL!!* Cashew later!

At the Head Scientist's home...

≷YAWN!≷ Gee, what a long day. My dogs are barkin'!

And by "dogs" I mean all those **HOT DOGS** I ate.

Oog.

gurgle

Time to get in my jammies. But first, to the bathroom, to drop these dogs off at the kennel!

AAAAAA

—lligators, correct.

You should really put a lock on your toilet lid, doctor. *Anyone* could get in this way!

142

I'm Brash and this is Mango. We're **InvestiGators**. Sorry for walking in on you like this.

Really, *he* walked in on *us*.

Doctor, what did you tell the badgers about PRIME ROBOT?

Hmm, I never talked to any badgers...

If they were questioning scientists at the Science Factory, it must have been when I was out shopping for replacement hot dog buns.

I wasn't gonna eat *BUN-LESS* hot dogs! I'm a *DOCTOR!*

Well, DOCTOR, this robot of yours is now a GHOST who's been *combining* your coworkers with **light meals!** And if we don't stop it, it might combine *YOU* next!

Did you say "combine"? That word rings a bell...

Yeah... It definitely strikes a chord...

Like...when we were undercover as musicians...

≥GASP!≤ **BRASH!** THE **COMBINOTRON CODE** from that rocket!

But...we destroyed the rocket. How could the combinotron code get into the robot?

I'm sorry, Mango... Before I pushed the self-destruct button... I pushed the **other** comically large... confusingly labelled...enormous... red button.

Push me!

NO, Push me!

Oh, yeeeaahh... I **DO** remember that...

I didn't realize it at the time, but I guess the rocket *did* transmit the **combinotron code**. And it *did* end up in the wrong hands...

PRIME ROBOT'S hands!

A **rocket** transmitted **combinotron code**? It must have been intercepted by the Science Factory's radar dishes and downloaded into Prime Robot's hugging subroutine. Which means...I had him plugged into the WRONG OUTLET! Oops. *Silly me!*

But this also explains why he went haywire when I told him to **hug** Dr. Morrow. Prime Robot's hands weren't built to handle the *raw power* of a **COMBINOTRON!**

So...how did Prime Robot become a ghost?

When the Science Factory flooded, he **short-circuited**. As far as robots go, that's as good as **dead!** But to come back as a *ghost?*

The ability to combine things wouldn't make him do *THAT.*

What if...when the robot *short-circuited* in the flood...the **COMBINOTRON** powers *backfired*... and *combined* PRIME ROBOT with the WATER?

THAT'S IT! *That's* why all the victims were wet!

Robot Ghost isn't a ghost— he just **LOOKS** like one. He's made of **water!** He's a *MIST!*

When we found Dr. Morrow, I thought he was all sweaty. And you accused Dr. Salad of using too much dressing.

Who eats a *DRY* salad, really?

But they were wet because the **misty menace** *passed through* them!

By **HUGGING** these people, the robo-mist made them *moist*, and the combinotron power *combined* them with whatever they were touching at the time.

Which, to remind anyone not keeping track, was a snake, a banana, and some mixed vegetables.

Add to that the fact that the robot is *ALSO* made of **electricity!**

So *THAT'S* how he's been coming out of electrical appliances. He can travel through the power lines!

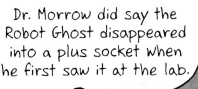

Dr. Morrow did say the Robot Ghost disappeared into a plus socket when he first saw it at the lab.

ELECTRIFIED MIST! It's so crazy it's the only thing that makes sense!

Doctor, we've **got** to find a way to stop your robot and uncombine these people. Can you think of any way to communicate with it? To get through to it?

Maybe... But what I'd need is back at the Science Factory!

Then let's get to it!

Nuh-uh, Doc.

?

We're takin' a shortcut...

click

WHAT is wrong with ME? What... What AM I?

Once again, viewers, beware of a **ROBOT GENIE** who comes out of electrical appliances...

...and **attacks** people while they're eating!

So if you're watching this during dinner...

...PUT DOWN THAT TACO!

Here again is the artist's rendering of this *transparent terror*... Which sort of looks like it may be a **ghost**? But that *lamp* is a clear sign that it's a **genie**, so I'm sticking with **ROBOT GENIE**. But the only wish *this* genie grants...*is a night in the hospital!*

And now, the weather...

Am I...a ROBOT *GENIE?* No. WISHES do not compute...

So if I am a ROBOT GHOST, am I...*DEAD?*

I just...

...Want to... HUG things...

Things like...those KIT—TENS over there...on that CEMENT MIX—ER...

zzt

KIT—TENS... HUG KIT—TENS...

I'm not here to hurt you...

I have an offer to make you...

You are a CRACK—ER...and also a CROCO—DILE... You are a...*CRACKER—DILE!*

YES! Thank you! It's *obviously* clever wordplay, right?

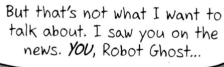

But that's not what I want to talk about. I saw you on the news. *YOU*, Robot Ghost...

...can *travel through power lines!*

Yes, I figured it out! I can put two and two together.

Can... *I* put two and two together?

Well, if you've figured out how you'll be of use to me – *I MEAN* – how you can **HELP** me, then yes.

Will there... be HUGS?

Um... Sure. There'll be *plenty* of hugs. **All the hugs you want!** Just, uh, not yet...

I am still but a brittle, twice-baked saltine cracker.

BEFORE the hugs, there's this THING I want you to get for me. Once I have that, my crumby carcass can handle hugs.

And I will finally be *stronger* than just a *saltine!*

Stronger like...a BAGEL?

No, something even *STRONGER!*

A stale PITA?

What? **NO!**

Really, really old CROUTONS?

Burned PIZZA CRUST?

NO, NO! Stop thinking bread products!

Uncooked PASTA?

Is it bigger than a BREAD BASK—ET?

JUST FOLLOW ME!

Morning, Mr. Septapus! Early bird gets the worm, eh?

Indeed!

Or in this case, the breakfast burrito!

Breakfast is the most important meal of the day, after all. See you later, Dave!

Bye...

...but my name is Steve.

What's this? *Hurm.*

Mango and Brash were supposed to have mopped up this level yesterday.

A.R.M.S.

Where ARE those Gators?

Ah! Marsha and Bongo! Have you seen Mango and/or Brash?

Well, **yes.** That's...why we're here.

We need new V.E.S.T.s — ones that we can be sure weren't tampered with by those... **InstiGators.**

Oh, perfect timing! I just finished a new V.E.S.T. prototype last night. I'm sure it will fit any—

ROBOT GHOST!

Well, I was going to say "occasion"...

He's stealing a V.E.S.T.!
STOP THAT GHOST!

Ehn! Ehn! Ehn!

I've...almost... got 'im...

Bongo!
BONGO!!

I'M Marsha!
YOU'RE Bongo!

Whatever!

Just see if you can reach the business card in my... lower...flap?

Oh!

After Prime Robot first malfunctioned, I realized the *weird code* I saw in his **hugging subroutine** must have been the cause. I tried *deleting* the code, but he had already been **unplugged** from this computer, so it had no effect.

Now, having learned it was **combinotron code**, I've discovered that the code *itself* will combine with *any other program* it encounters.

It combined with Prime Robot's hugging program, and now his hugs combine things. So, how do we stop it?

Now that I know what code I'm looking at, I can rewrite Prime Robot's main programming so that it **separates** the combinotron code from his hugging subroutine.

That will take the combinotron powers **out** of his hands, and he'll no longer combine things by hugging them.

The trick will be finding a way to get him to download this new data. In his gaseous form, we can't just plug him into a computer.

He's a *mist*. Can't we just...upload to the cloud?

Hmm... If *hugs* caused **HIM** to combine with **WATER**... Can you invent a way for him to *hug* the **DATA?**

We heard you designed him with true human emotions. Maybe if we appeal to—

bleep blurp

163

Oh, hey, someone's trying to contact the B-Team.

bleep blurp

That's odd... The signal's coming from inside S.U.I.T. headquarters!

CARD LOCATION

Turn on the video feed!

It **IS** the **B-TEAM!** Bongo and/or Marsha!

Mango! Brash! A V.E.S.T. has been stolen from the A.R.M.S. Division!

WHAT?! Did Crackerdile manage to break in?!

NO, it was **ROBOT GHOST!**

And only *YOU* can stop him, InvestiGators!

But...*why?* How would Robot Ghost know about S.U.I.T.? *Or* our V.E.S.T.s?

I bet it **WAS** Crackerdile! Even using the sewers, he could *never* get in and out of S.U.I.T. as easily as a **mist** that can travel through plug sockets could! He must have convinced Robot Ghost to *steal* a V.E.S.T. *for* him!

≥GASP!≥

Prime Robot has become... **CRIME ROBOT!**

Luckily, just like C-ORB, every V.E.S.T. has a **tracking device** installed. But we'll have to find it before Crackerdile gets his crumby claws on it and turns the tracker off!

Doctor! We need a way to get the new code into Prime Robot! You've got to invent harder than you've ever invented before!

Cue the *scientific inventing montage!*

We don't have **time** for a montage! Let's just turn the page to where it's *finished!*

IT'S FINISHED!

I think? It's hard to tell, since we skipped all those pages that would've shown me building it.

Then there's no time to lose! *Let's follow that V.E.S.T.!*

V.E.S.T. TRAKR

VPP

VPP

Boop

SCIENCE FACTORY

Soon...

Psst! Over here!

No, behind the bush!

What? **NO**, not in the *sky!*

Ah, forget it.

Robot Ghost, give me the V.E.S.T.!

I can have HUG now?

Wish? I did not **WISH** for this, *GENIE* or not!

Almost...

...THERE!

beep

Hello, Prime Robot!

...Gramma?

VVRRP

Yes, Prime Robot. I am your **HOLOGRAMMA**.

Prime Robot has a holographic grandmother?

Shh! Don't ruin the moment!

Gramma... I just want to HUG—MORE... But people *run* from me...and then I COM—BINE them...and they *hate* me...

Nobody hates you, Prime Robot.

Am I...capable of LOVE? Or even...BEING loved?

You ARE loved, Prime Robot! **I** love you.

Now tell me... Do you accept cookies?

YES NO

Oh, YES!

Brash, why'd you hold me back? Now *NOTHING* can stop Crackerdile!

Give it time, Mango.

You Gators are all washed up! **Just like when I flooded the city!** And— *What the?*

Why—why am I all **WET?!** I'm melting... *MELTING!*

Oh! **HE'S** the one who's all *washed up!*

Crackerdile didn't realize Robot Ghost is made of water. The moisture just had to **SOAK IN** for him to get all **MUSHY** on us.

NO! This isn't over!

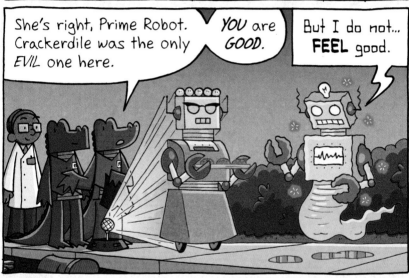

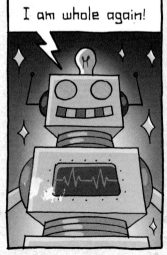

I...FEEL better now. I can sense my emotional programming and the COMBINOTRON code are no longer in conflict. Thank you.

You're welcome, Prime Robot. And now...

...Goodbye!

Beep

vvrrp

AAAH!! Did you just DELETE him?!

No, of course not! I just turned him off. Prime Robot — or Prime ROBOGRAM, I should say — exists entirely intact within this hologram projector.

What happened to his grandmother? His hologramma?

She's a part of him now. But, in a way, she already was.

To create Prime Robot's **true human emotions**, I based his programming on *family relationships*... Parents, grandparents, siblings – even pets!

That's what made his urge to **HUG** so *powerful!*

As we eventually figured out, combinotron code got **mixed in** with his hugging subroutine, forcing him to *COMBINE* whatever he tried hugging!

The only way to fix that mix-up was to write a *new* version of his main program. That part was easy. But since Prime Robot had gotten himself combined with water, turning him into what everyone thought was a Robot Ghost, the *real* challenge was **how** to get the new data into him.

When Brash suggested that we could implant the new programming in Robot Ghost by having him somehow **HUG** the data, it gave me an idea!

Apparently, during the montage we skipped, I invented **this device**, which could *project* the new programming as a *hologram*.

Then it just became a question of making the holographic data appear as something — or some*ONE* — Robot Ghost would **want** to hug.

Thinking back to Prime Robot's original programming, the answer was clear: I could make the code look like his gramma! And *who* can resist a hug from their *gramma*? **Especially** when she has cookies!

WOW! Who knew *robotics* had so much **emotional manipulation!**

Well, the day is saved, moistly.

I mean, "mostly."

But there's still work to do! Let's get that V.E.S.T. back to S.U.I.T. and see if there's a way to cure Robot Ghost's victims. Come on!

Chapter ONE MILLION (or thereabouts)

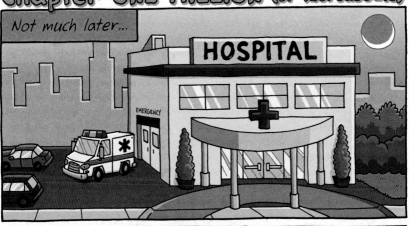

Not much later...

HOSPITAL

EMERGENCY

WOOP WOOP

A crash alert in the I.C.U.!

The **BANANA** and side **SALAD** combo — *I MEAN* — patients!

Cured? But...*how* is this possible?

Hey-o!

GATORS!

INT
CAR

And friends!

Ah. I didn't see you all there.

INT
CA

You see, Doc, Robot Ghost could COMBINE people with THINGS, because *he* was combined with **combinotron code** that...

...combined with *water*... and short-circuited... *something*...and there was a *rocket* at some point...

Trying to explain this is giving me a *headache!*

Do you need a brain surgeon?

I can take care of this ache. *I'm* the **HEAD Scientist!**

I was able to *reprogram* the entity formerly known as Robot Ghost — who now exists as a hologram.

I *reversed* his combinotron powers, and turned them into **UNCOMBINOTRON** powers!

With the use of this holographic projector, the new and improved **Prime Robogram** was able to *uncombine* these patients from their low-protein dinners and restore them to normal!

So delicious!

So dry!

It uncombined **us** as well! We're no longer badgers!

You mean "badges."

That's what I said.

No, you said "badgers."

Would that thing work on...**ANY** combination? Like, say, a **brain surgeon** and a **news helicopter?**

That's a good question.

So far, it's only been used to **uncombinotron** things that were **combinotronned.** I'd recommend more testing before using it to undo combinations made by *other* means.

Why, you know someone?

Uh, just asking for a friend.

Well, it *should* work on... THE SNAKE-ARMED PLUMBER WHO'S STILL MISSING!

You mean you haven't found him?!

HEY! *We* aren't even on *active duty*. *YOU TWO* were supposed to solve this case!

Uh, we were turned into badges! And, um...you guys are the *A-team*... You know, *A* for...*Awesome...?* *Astonishing?*

And we're the *B-team*, for, uh—

Wouldn't he want to see if a doctor could get the snake off his arm?

Is the *snake* on the *PLUMBER?* Or is the *plumber* on the *SNAKE?*

What's the difference?

Well, all the *other* combinations Robot Ghost created were with **fruits** and **vegetables**. Which, as far as science can tell, don't have minds of their own.

But a plumber does!

He means the snake.

Oh, right.

So the question is... which **MIND** is in control? The *PLUMBER'S?* Or the *SNAKE'S?*

THUD!

Huff
Huff

W-where am I? How long have I been...swinging around the city?

And what's **happened** to me? My arm...and *Slinker*, my drain snake tool...and that *REAL* snake... have **COMBINED**...into...a grappling hook?

Like some...
some...

But you and your arm can be the *first* to join my army!

We're *lisssssssstening...*

Bill

First, do me a solid and scoop me up into that bucket over there.

Blorp

Ah, *MUCH* better.

Now, let me tell you a tale... A tale of a team... A team called... **T.A.I.L.BLAZERS!**

Epilogue

Leaving your posts... Interfering with the B-Team's investigation... *HACKING* into the **S.U.I.T.** business card network?!

Mango and **Brash**, I have *NO CHOICE* but to **suspend** you from S.U.I.T. *PERMANENTLY!*

Then again, you *DID* rescue C-ORB, stop **Robot Ghost**, recover the stolen **V.E.S.T.**, *and* get **Crackerdile** to admit to flooding the city while possibly disposing of him *for good.*

AND you brought me these **warm socks**, fresh from the dryer!

So I have *NO CHOICE* but to promote you to the ranks you had before.

Well, I *DO* have a choice... But I *WANT* to!

Welcome *back* to S.U.I.T., InvestiGators!

Now, go away, so I can try on these socks!

And get yourselves new V.E.S.T.s!

Thanks, General Inspector!

The **secret sewer system** entrances to S.U.I.T. have all been *rearranged* and *rerouted*. So S.O.U.P.'s off!

That should keep Crackerdile out for good, even if he *does* find a way to pull himself back together.

That's hard to imagine. There wasn't much left of him.

There's ONLY mush left of him!

Still, I can't help but wonder if there's any part of my former partner, Daryl, left at all.

If we learned *anything* from this adventure, Brash, it's that people can change. They can change into foods AND back! Maybe there's still hope for Daryl.

The Secret Agent word of the day is: ACCOMPLICE

Robot Ghost stole a V.E.S.T. from S.U.I.T., but he isn't the only one responsible for the crime. Crackerdile was his **accomplice**.

According to S.U.I.T.PEDIA, an **accomplice** is someone who helps someone else in a criminal activity.

Keep an eye out for MANGO & BRASH'S next adventure!

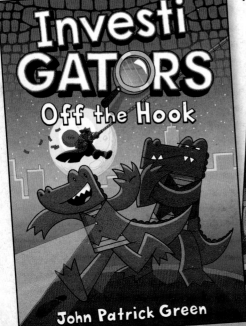

Investi GATORS
Off the Hook
John Patrick Green

And be sure to read where their adventures began!

Investi GATORS
John Patrick Green

Special thanks to...

Aaron Polk and his flatters, Christine Brunson, Robin Fasel, and Rowan Westmoreland, for their amazing colors.
The usual suspects at First Second, especially my editors, Calista Brill and Rachel Stark.
Jen Linnan, my (secret) agent and demolitions expert.
Jon Roscetti, for the printer ink.
My brother, Bill, for introducing me to comic books.
Dave Roman, for reintroducing me to comic books.
And my parents, for never discouraging me from drawing.

John Patrick Green is a human with the human job of making books about animals with human jobs, such as *Hippopotamister*, the Kitten Construction Company series, and now the InvestiGators series. John is definitely not just a bunch of animals wearing a human suit pretending to have a human job. He is also the artist and co-creator of the graphic novel series Teen Boat!, with writer Dave Roman. John lives in Brooklyn in an apartment that doesn't allow animals other than the ones living in his head.